U0025441

Hercules

Welcome to the World of Mythology

Mythology gives you interesting explanations about life and satisfies your curiosity with stories that have been made up to explain surprising or frightening phenomena.

People throughout the world have their own myths. In the imaginary world of mythology, humans can become birds or stars. The sun, wind, trees, and the rest of the natural world are full of gods who often interact with humans.

Greek and Roman mythology began more than 3,000 years ago. It consisted of stories first told by Greeks that lived on the shores of the Mediterranean Sea. In Italy the Romans would later borrow and modify many of these stories.

Most of the Greek myths were related to gods that resided upon the cloud-shrouded Mount Olympus. These clouds frequently could create a mysterious atmosphere on Mount

Olympus. The ancient Greeks thought that their gods dwelt there and had human shapes, feelings, and behavior.

The Greeks and the Romans built temples, offered animal sacrifices, said prayers, performed plays, and competed in sports to please their humanlike gods on Mount Olympus.

How the world came into being in the first place?
Why is there night and day?
How did the four seasons come into existence?
Where do we go after we die?

Reading Greek and Roman mythology can help us understand the early human conceptions of the world. Since many Western ideas originated with the Greeks and Romans, you will benefit from taking a look into the mythology that helped to shape those ancient cultures. Understanding their mythology will give you an interesting view of the world you live in.

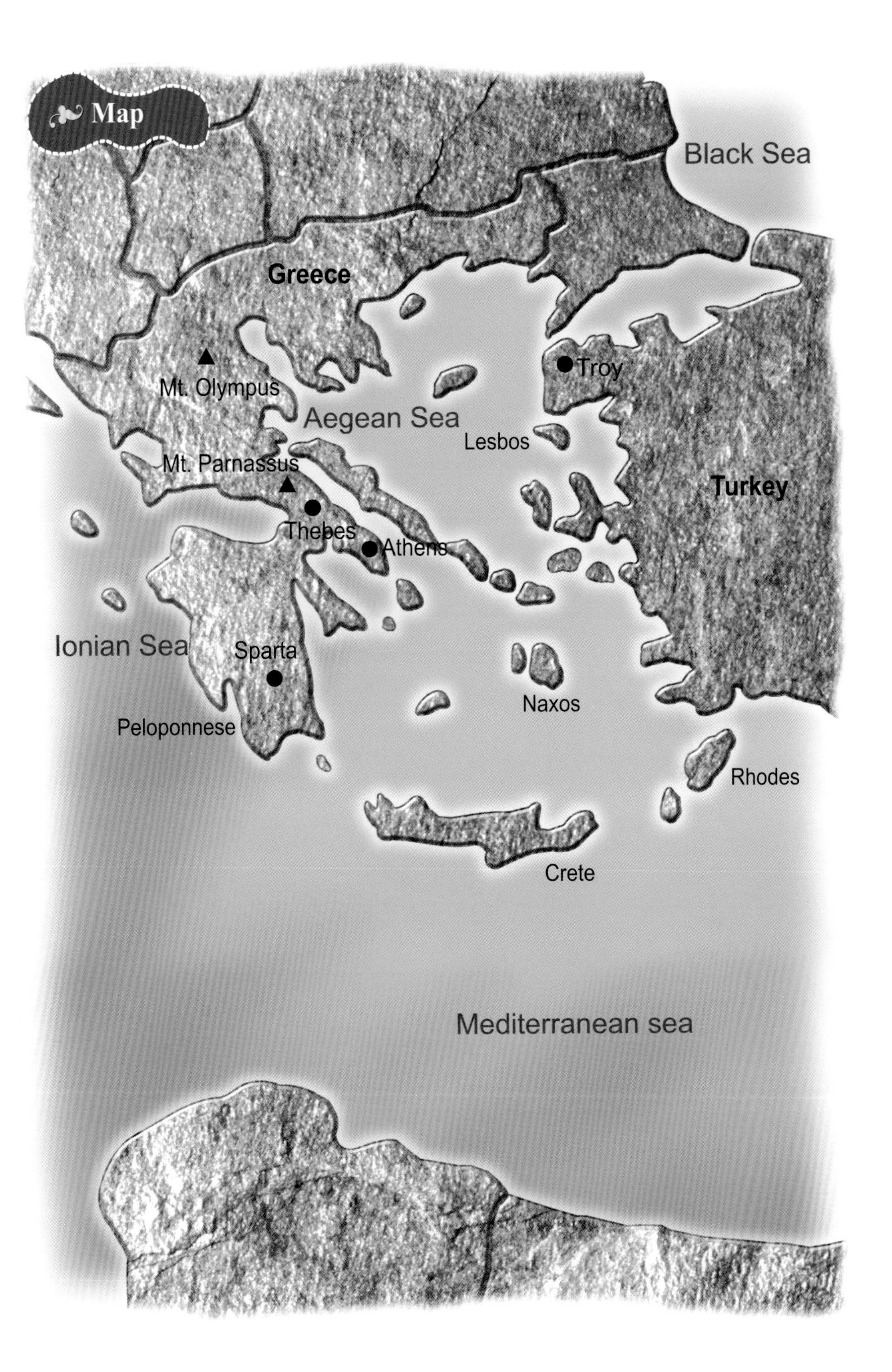
Map
Black Sea
Greece
Troy
Mt. Olympus
Aegean Sea
Lesbos
Mt. Parnassus
Turkey
Thebes
Athens
Ionian Sea
Sparta
Naxos
Peloponnese
Rhodes
Crete
Mediterranean sea

Before Reading *Hercules*

Hercules is best known as the strongest hero in Greek mythology. He was the son of the god Zeus and an earth woman Alcmene. As the first child between the most powerful god and a human, from the very moment of his birth, Hercules was very special.

Zeus' wife, Hera despised Hercules for being born between her husband and another woman so much that she even tried to kill Hercules by sending serpents to him. However, Hercules had such great strength even as a baby that he was able to strangle the snakes. Despite Hera's animosity, Hercules grew up healthily. And he lived happily in marriage, raising children with a beautiful woman, Megara.

But one day, Hera put a curse on Hercules, which drove him insane, and in his madness he killed not only his wife and children, but also many other people. After he had recovered his sanity, he was overwhelmed with guilt and fear. Hera, who wanted to harass Hercules more, made him go and visit King Eurystheus. King Eurystheus instructed Hercules to undertake as many as twelve nearly-impossible tasks, which is known as the famous '12 labors of Hercules'.

We will see how Hercules completed such impossible tasks in the next pages.

The characters in the stories

Hercules
The Greek hero who has to perform 12 labors, under Hera's curse.

Hera
The queen of gods. She curses Hercules.

Eurystheus
The king of Tiryns who gives 12 labors.

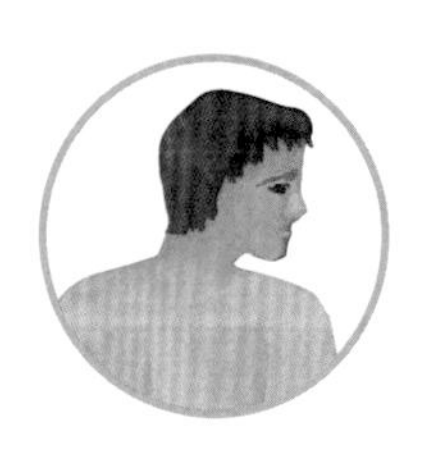

Lolaus
Hercules' assistant who helps Hercules kill Hydra.

Minos
The king of Crete. Hercules helps the king to kill the bull that the god of the sea Poseidon sent to king Minos.

Hyppolyta
The queen of the Amazons who gives her girdle to Hercules.

Atlas
One of Titans. He carries the Earth upon his two shoulders.

Contents

Hercules the Hero

01

Hercules was a famous Greek hero.
His mother was Alcmena,
a human princess.
His father was Zeus, the king of the gods.
So Hercules had special powers.

One day, the goddess Hera sent two snakes.
She wanted to kill Hercules.
But he killed the snakes.

Hercules grew older.
He did many great things.
He was a very good shot with a bow and arrow.
He was the strongest man in the world.
Hercules married a beautiful woman named Megara.
Megara, Hercules, and their children
were very happy together.

02

The goddess Hera hated Hercules.
She wanted bad luck for Hercules.
One night, she used bad magic on Hercules.
The magic made him crazy.
Suddenly he killed his wife, children,
and many other people.

Three days later, Hercules became normal again. He was very upset. Hercules prayed to the gods. And he asked them for help.

But Hera wanted to hurt Hercules more. "Hercules, go to the land of King Eurystheus. You will work for him there," Hera said.

Twelve Labors of Hercules

03

Hercules arrived at Eurystheus's kingdom.
"Hello, King Eurystheus," said Hercules,
"I have to do everything you say."
King Eurystheus thought Hercules wanted
to kill him and be a king.
So he thought for a long time.

The king said, "You must do
twelve labors for me.
When you finish them,
I'll set you free again."

"What is the first labor?"
Hercules asked.
"There is a lion in the valley of Nemea,"
said the king.
"The lion is killing many people.
So it must be killed.
Bring me the skin of the Nemean lion."

Hercules traveled to the valley of Nemea.
People warned Hercules not to come close
to the lion.
But Hercules did not give up.

Hercules finally found the lion.

The Nemean lion was a huge animal.

It made a big noise and ran at Hercules.

Hercules hit the lion many times with his club.

But it didn't work.

Hercules used his hands instead.

Then, he was able to kill the lion.

Hercules returned.

The people shouted for joy.

The people cheered Hercules

because he killed the lion.

But King Eurystheus was very surprised.

"Hercules killed the lion?

Hmm, how did he do that?"

Hercules and the Nemean Lion

05

Finally, Hercules came to the castle.
"What is the second labor?" he asked.
"You must go to the country of Argos.
There you'll find the Hydra.
The Hydra is a monster with nine heads.
You, Hercules, must find the Hydra and kill it,"
the king ordered.

This time, Hercules traveled with his helper, Iolaus.
They traveled for a long time.
Finally, they found the land of Argos.
The huge Hydra quickly ran at Hercules.
Hercules hit the Hydra's heads with his club.
He knocked off one head.
But two more heads grew in its place.
Soon, the Hydra had twenty heads.
But Hercules was not afraid.

06

“Iolaus, bring fire quickly!”

Hercules called out.

He knocked off one of the heads.

Then, Iolaus burned the neck with the fire.

The heads stopped growing back.

Finally, there was only one more head.

“This head will not die. It cannot be killed,” said Hercules.

Then, he lifted up a huge rock.

He threw it at the Hydra.

The rock hit the Hydra’s head.

It buried the Hydra.

Eurystheus was very surprised.

“Next, you must catch the Cerynitian deer,” said Eurystheus.

The deer had golden horns.
And it was a pet of the goddess Artemis.
Hercules found the deer in the forest.
But it wasn’t easy to catch it.
After one year, he caught the deer.

Artemis and Her Deer

08

"Next, bring me the Erymanthian boar.
Bring it to me alive."
The Erymanthian boar was a very
dangerous animal.
It killed farmers and damaged the crops.
Hercules fought with the boar.
The boar ran away and stopped
at a snowy mountain.
So Hercules grabbed the boar.
He took it to Eurystheus alive.

09

'What can I have Hercules do next?'
Eurystheus thought,
'I must give him a job he cannot do.'

"Hercules, you must go to
the land of King Augeas.
King Augeas has over three thousand oxen.
His stables are the largest in the world.
No one cleaned them for thirty years.
You must clean the stables in one day."

Hercules arrived at the land of King Augeas.
Then he looked at the stables.
"Phew! This is the worst thing.
The smell is terrible," he said.
He sat down to think.
'How can I clean
these stables?'
Then he had an idea.
"Aha! That's it!
I can use the rivers!"
he cried out.

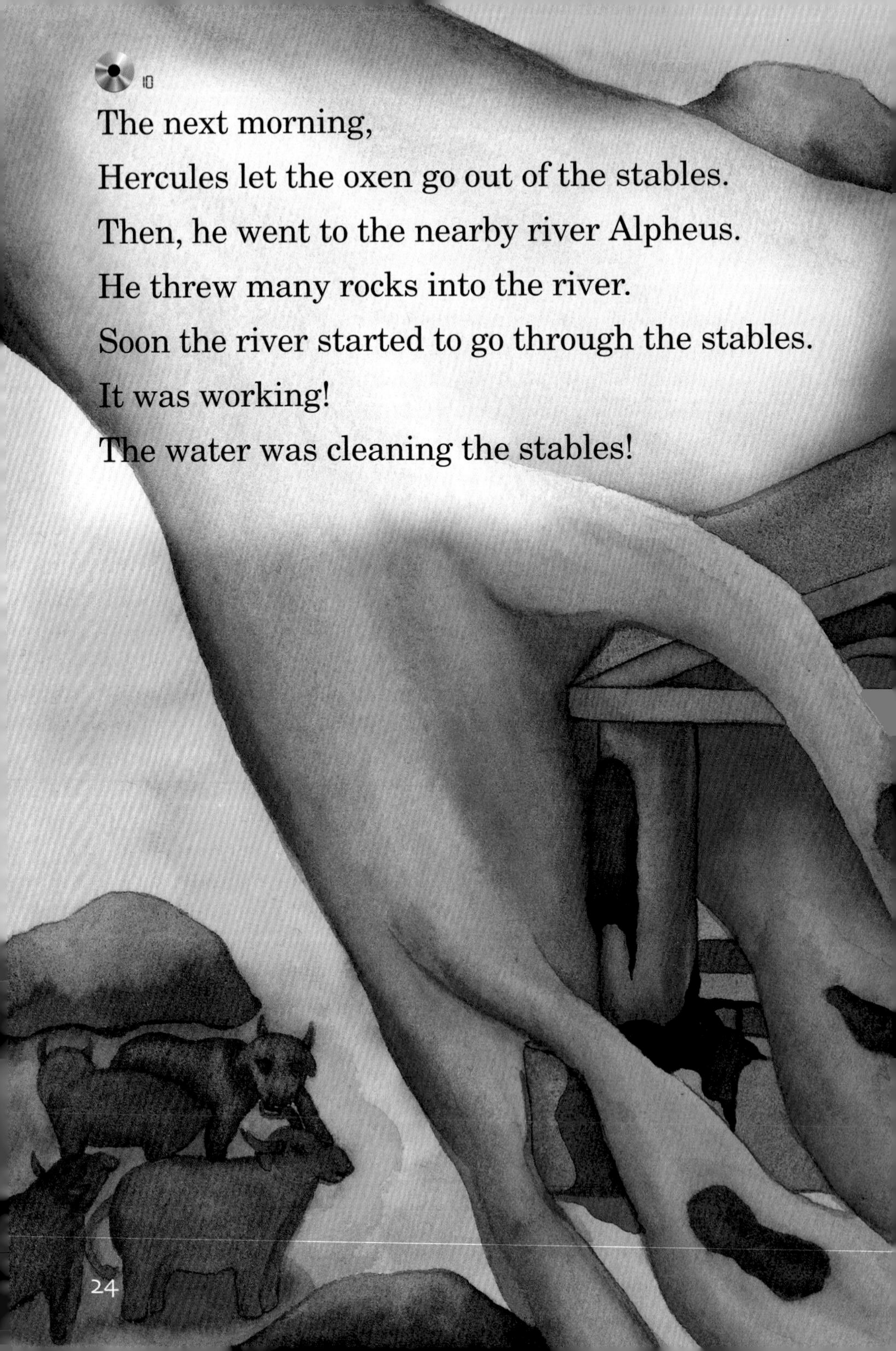

10

The next morning,

Hercules let the oxen go out of the stables.

Then, he went to the nearby river Alpheus.

He threw many rocks into the river.

Soon the river started to go through the stables.

It was working!

The water was cleaning the stables!

But it was not enough.
The stables were very big.
So Hercules needed more water.
He went to the river Peneus.
He threw rocks into that river, too.
Soon, water from both rivers was flowing into the stables.
By the end of the day, the stables were clean.

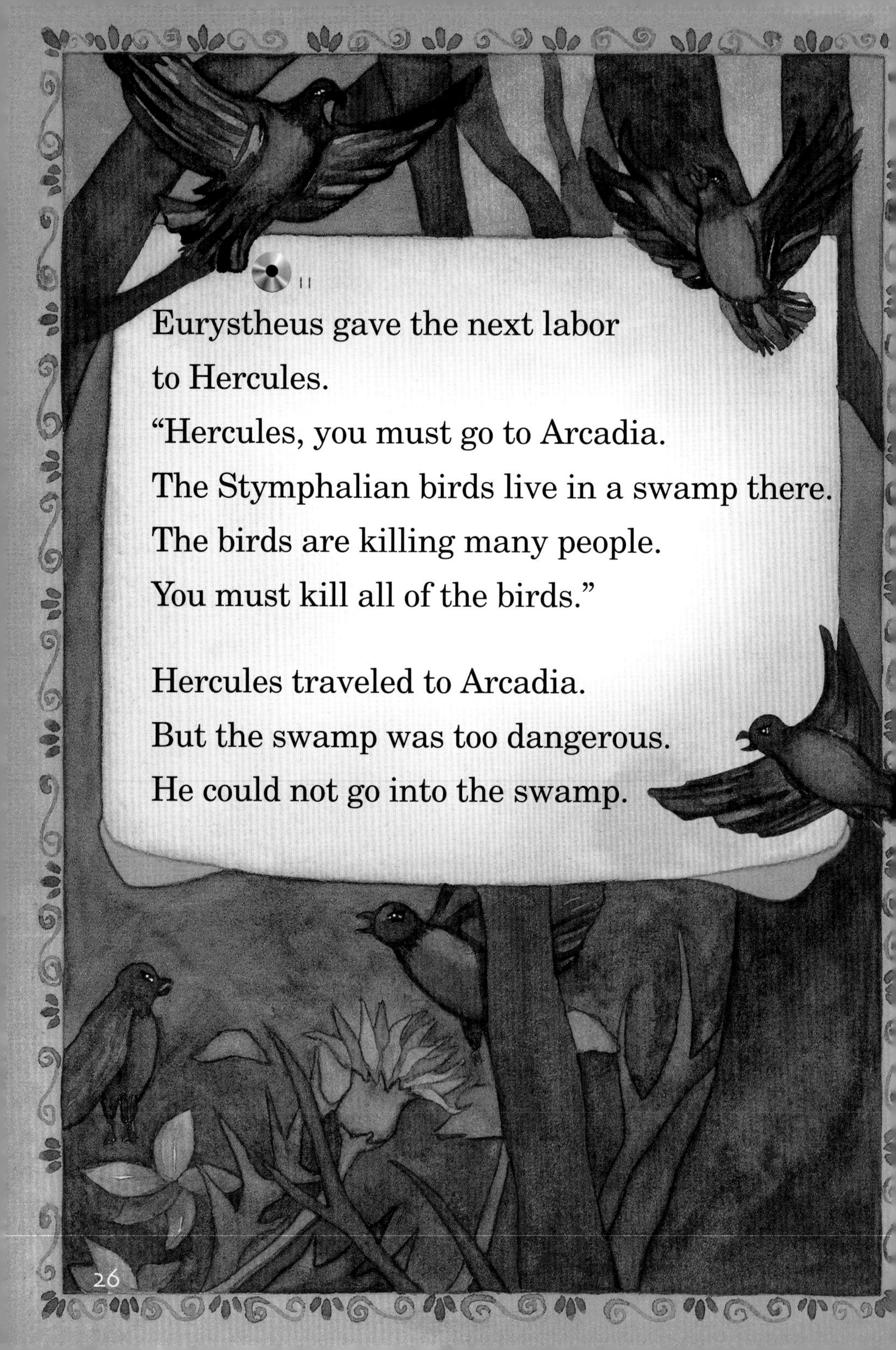

11

Eurystheus gave the next labor
to Hercules.
"Hercules, you must go to Arcadia.
The Stymphalian birds live in a swamp there.
The birds are killing many people.
You must kill all of the birds."

Hercules traveled to Arcadia.
But the swamp was too dangerous.
He could not go into the swamp.

Suddenly, the goddess
Athena came to Hercules.
Athena wanted to help him.
She gave him a drum.
"Play the drum.
Then the birds will fly away.
When they fly in the air,
you can kill all of them."

12

Hercules played the drum loudly.
The Stymphalian birds hated the noise.
They flew up into the air.
The birds flew at Hercules.
They were very angry.
Hercules took out his bow and arrow.
Then, he shot all of the birds.
He finished his sixth labor.

Hercules returned
to King Eurystheus.
"Hercules," said Eurystheus,
"King Minos needs you.
There is a bull on the island of Crete.
The bull is the father of the Minotaur.
The Minotaur is a bad monster.
And the bull is also very bad.
It is scaring many people."

King Minos and Hercules traveled together.
“There is the bull,” said King Minos,
“Please, Hercules. Take it away from Crete.”
Hercules chased the bull.
And the bull fought Hercules.
The bull even breathed fire at Hercules.
But he caught the bull.
And he took it away from Crete.

Hercules Fighting with the Bull

Later, Eurystheus asked Hercules
for the horses of Diomedes.
These horses did not eat grass or oats.
They ate people.
Hercules asked Diomedes for the horses.
"No! You can not have my horses,"
Diomedes said.
So Hercules and Diomedes fought.
But Hercules won.

15

His next labor was very difficult.
Hercules had to go to the land of the Amazons.
The Amazons were a nation of women.
There were no men in the land.
He had to return with the belt of their queen.
He took a small group of heroes with him.
They sailed for a long time.

Did you know?  16

The Amazons

The Amazons were a tribe of women.
The Greeks said that the Amazons were
very brave women warriors.
They used bows and arrows to fight.
Sometimes they used spears.
It was their custom to raise only female children.
Boys were either sent away or killed.
They worshiped Ares as their 'god of war'
and Artemis as their 'goddess of female power.'

Hercules and his men finally found the Amazons.
"No men may enter our land," said the Amazons.

"I must speak to your queen,"
said Hercules,
"Please take us to your queen."
The Amazons looked at Hercules.
He looked very strong and brave.
So they brought him
to their queen,
Hippolyta.

“Why did you come to my land, Hercules?”
Hippolyta asked.
“I have to bring back your belt,” he answered.
Hippolyta liked brave Hercules.
So she gave him her belt.
However, the goddess Hera was very angry.
She tricked the other Amazons.
“Hercules is taking Hippolyta
to his boat,” said Hera.

The Amazons believed
Hera's lie.
There was a great battle down near
Hercules's ship.
Even Queen Hippolyta was killed in the fight.
Hercules was very sad. He liked Hippolyta.
But he had her belt.
So he returned to the castle of King Eurystheus.

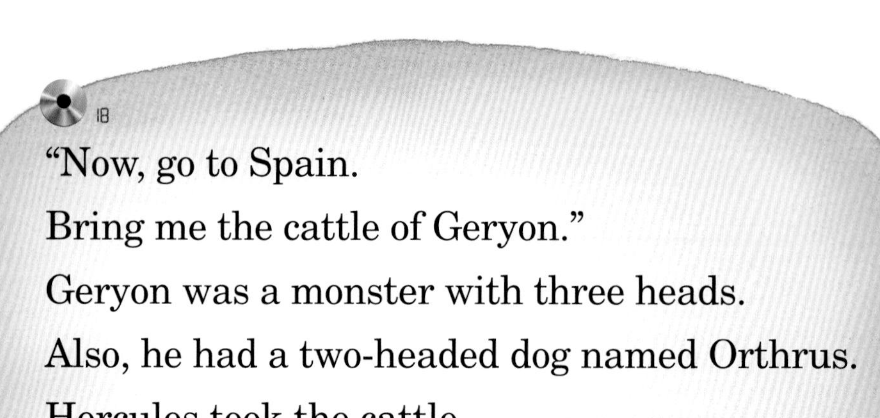

"Now, go to Spain.
Bring me the cattle of Geryon."
Geryon was a monster with three heads.
Also, he had a two-headed dog named Orthrus.
Hercules took the cattle.
Geryon and Orthrus ran after him.
But Hercules killed both of them.
He finally went back to Greece with the cattle.

19

"Next, bring me
the apples of the Hesperides,"
he ordered.
The Hesperides were nymphs.
They kept many magical apples.
And they were Hera's.
A dragon was watching the apples.
Hercules asked many people about the apples.
One person said,
"Ask Atlas. He knows."

Atlas was a Titan.
He held the world on his shoulders.
Hercules asked him for the apples.
"Okay, but you must hold the world for me," said Atlas. So Hercules held up the world.

Later, Atlas came back with the apples.
But Atlas did not want to hold it again.
Because the world was very heavy.

Hercules Holding the World

"Okay, I will hold the world," Hercules said.
"But I need a cushion.
Can you hold the world for me for one minute?
First, I will find a cushion.
Then, I will hold the world again."
Atlas held the world for Hercules.
"Thank you, Atlas," Hercules said.
Then he left with the apples.

"This is your last labor, Hercules," said Eurystheus,
"Go to Hades. Bring me the dog Cerberus."
Hades was the god of the underworld.
Cerberus was the guard dog of Hades.
Hercules came to the River Styx.
Only dead people could cross the River Styx.
But the ferryman was afraid of Hercules.
So Hercules could cross the river.

Then he found Cerberus.

Cerberus was a very big dog with three heads.

Its tail was a big snake.

And there were many snakes on its back.

Cerberus tried to bite Hercules.

But Hercules had his lion skin.

The lion skin was too strong.

So he was okay.

Hercules and Cerberus fought for a long, long time. Then, Cerberus became tired. Hercules won.
He took Cerberus across the River Styx.
Then he took Cerberus to Eurystheus.
“Here is Cerberus.
My labors are finished,” said Hercules.
“You may go now, Hercules.”

21

The Pillars of Hercules

Hercules came to the place where
Africa and Europe meet.
There he dug
into the earth
and made
two mountains.
The two mountains were called
"The Pillars of Hercules."
The mountain on the Spanish side was called Calpe.
The other mountain, on the African side,
was called Abyla.

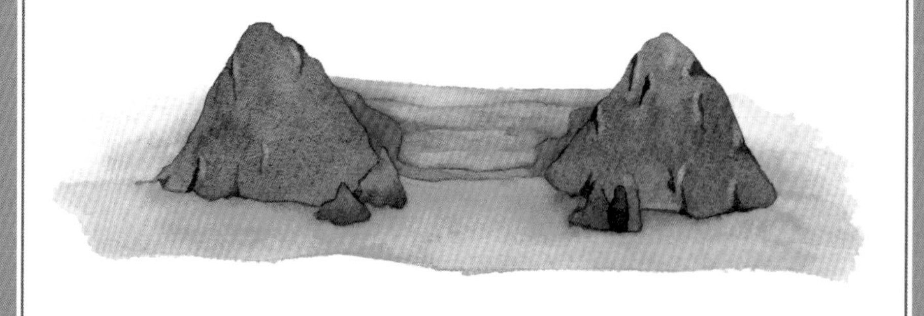

Another story says that there was one huge mountain before Hercules came.

He broke this mountain into two pieces.

Then the water from the Mediterranean could go between the mountains into the Atlantic.

Reading Comprehension

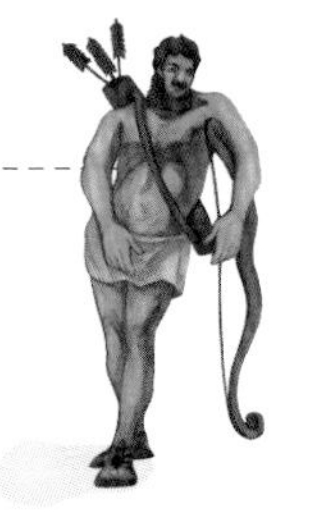

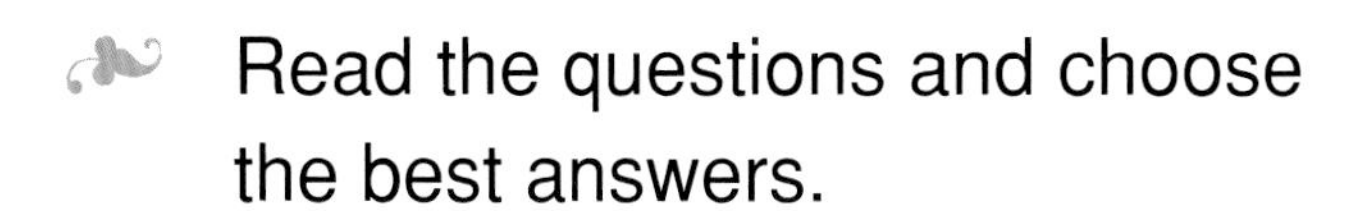

Read the questions and choose the best answers.

1. Circle True or False.

■ Hercules's mother is the goddess Hera.

True False

■ Hercules killed a lion when he was a baby.

True False

■ Hercules killed his children and wife.

True False

2. Which goddess did not like Hercules?

(A) Aphrodite (B) Artemis

(C) Athena (D) Hera

3. How many labors did Hercules have to do?

(A) 10 (B) 11 (C) 12 (D) 13

4. How did Hercules clean the King Augeas's stables?

(A) The gods helped him.
(B) He cleaned them with a bucket.
(C) He used two rivers.
(D) He didn't clean the stables.

5. What did Athena give Hercules?

(A) a drum (B) a xylophone
(C) a triangle (D) a piano

6. Circle True or False.

- Hercules killed the Erymanthian boar.

  True False

- The Amazons were all men.

  True False

- Cerberus was a snake with three heads.

  True False

7. What did Hercules bring back from the Amazons?

(A) a club (B) a lion
(C) a belt (D) a drum

8. Write the correct answer in the blank.

- The _______ of Diomedes did not eat grass of oats.

  They ate ___________.

- Atlas was a __________.

  He held the _______ on his shoulders.

9. What didn't Hercules kill?

(A) the Nemean lion
(B) the Hydra
(C) the King Augeas's oxen
(D) the Stymphalian birds

希臘羅馬神話故事 ❹

大力士海克力斯 Hercules

First Published March, 2011
First Printing March, 2011

Original Story by Thomas Bulfinch
Rewritten by Jeff Zeter
Illustrated by Imsoo Lee
Designer: Eonju No
Translated by Jia-chen Chuo

Printed and distributed by Cosmos Culture Ltd.
Tel: 02-2365-9739
Fax: 02-2365-9835
http://www.icosmos.com.tw
Publisher: Value-Deliver Culture Ltd.

Hercules

中譯解答本

卓加真　譯

歡迎來到神話的世界

神話用有趣的方式說明生命，各種故事解釋各種奇異或可怕現象，滿足人們的好奇心。世界上的每個民族，都有自己的神話。在神話的奇幻世界裡，人類可以化身成鳥或星辰。太陽、風、樹木等等，自然界萬物皆充滿了和人類互動頻繁的神靈。

希臘和羅馬神話的出現，已超過三千年，源自居住在地中海岸的希臘人。之後，再由義大利的羅馬人所接受，並進一步改寫之。

希臘神話的故事，大都與雲霄上的奧林帕斯山諸神有關。雲霧常爲奧林帕斯山蒙上神祕的氣氛，古希臘人認爲，神明就住在山上，其形體、感情和行爲舉止，無異於人。希臘人和羅馬人建立寺廟、獻祭動物、祈禳，並用戲劇和運動競賽的方式，來取悅那些住在奧林帕斯山、與人同形同性的眾神。

世界最初是如何形成的？
爲什麼會有晝夜之分？
爲什麼會有四季變化？
人死後將從何而去？

閱讀希臘羅馬神話，可以幫助我們瞭解早期人類的世界觀。又因許多西方思想乃源自於希臘人和羅馬人，故窺視希臘羅馬神話，將有助於塑造出那些古文化的眞貌。瞭解這些神話的內容，將可以讓人們對這個世界別有一番趣解。

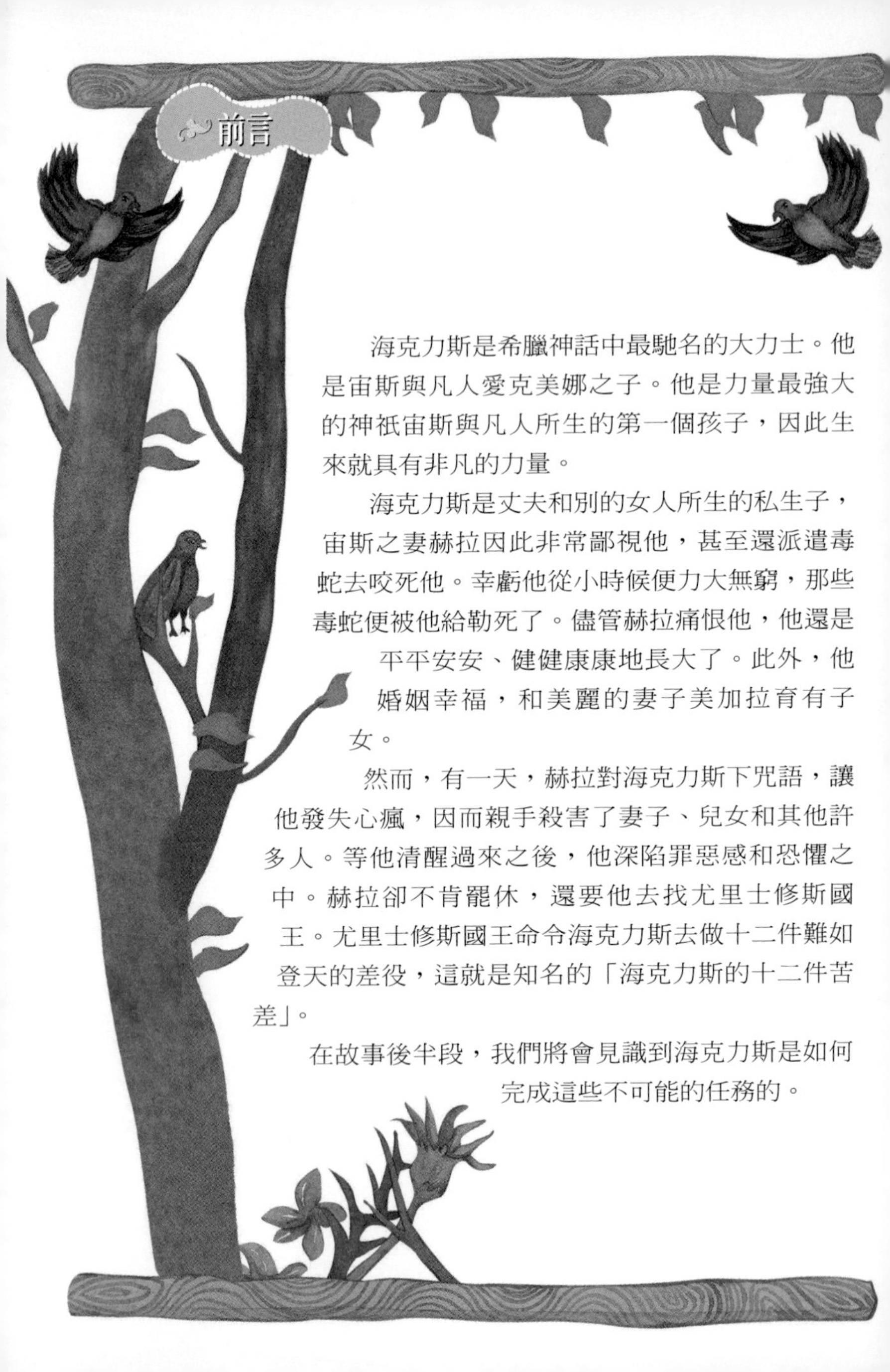

前言

海克力斯是希臘神話中最馳名的大力士。他是宙斯與凡人愛克美娜之子。他是力量最強大的神祇宙斯與凡人所生的第一個孩子，因此生來就具有非凡的力量。

海克力斯是丈夫和別的女人所生的私生子，宙斯之妻赫拉因此非常鄙視他，甚至還派遣毒蛇去咬死他。幸虧他從小時候便力大無窮，那些毒蛇便被他給勒死了。儘管赫拉痛恨他，他還是平平安安、健健康康地長大了。此外，他婚姻幸福，和美麗的妻子美加拉育有子女。

然而，有一天，赫拉對海克力斯下咒語，讓他發失心瘋，因而親手殺害了妻子、兒女和其他許多人。等他清醒過來之後，他深陷罪惡感和恐懼之中。赫拉卻不肯罷休，還要他去找尤里士修斯國王。尤里士修斯國王命令海克力斯去做十二件難如登天的差役，這就是知名的「海克力斯的十二件苦差」。

在故事後半段，我們將會見識到海克力斯是如何完成這些不可能的任務的。

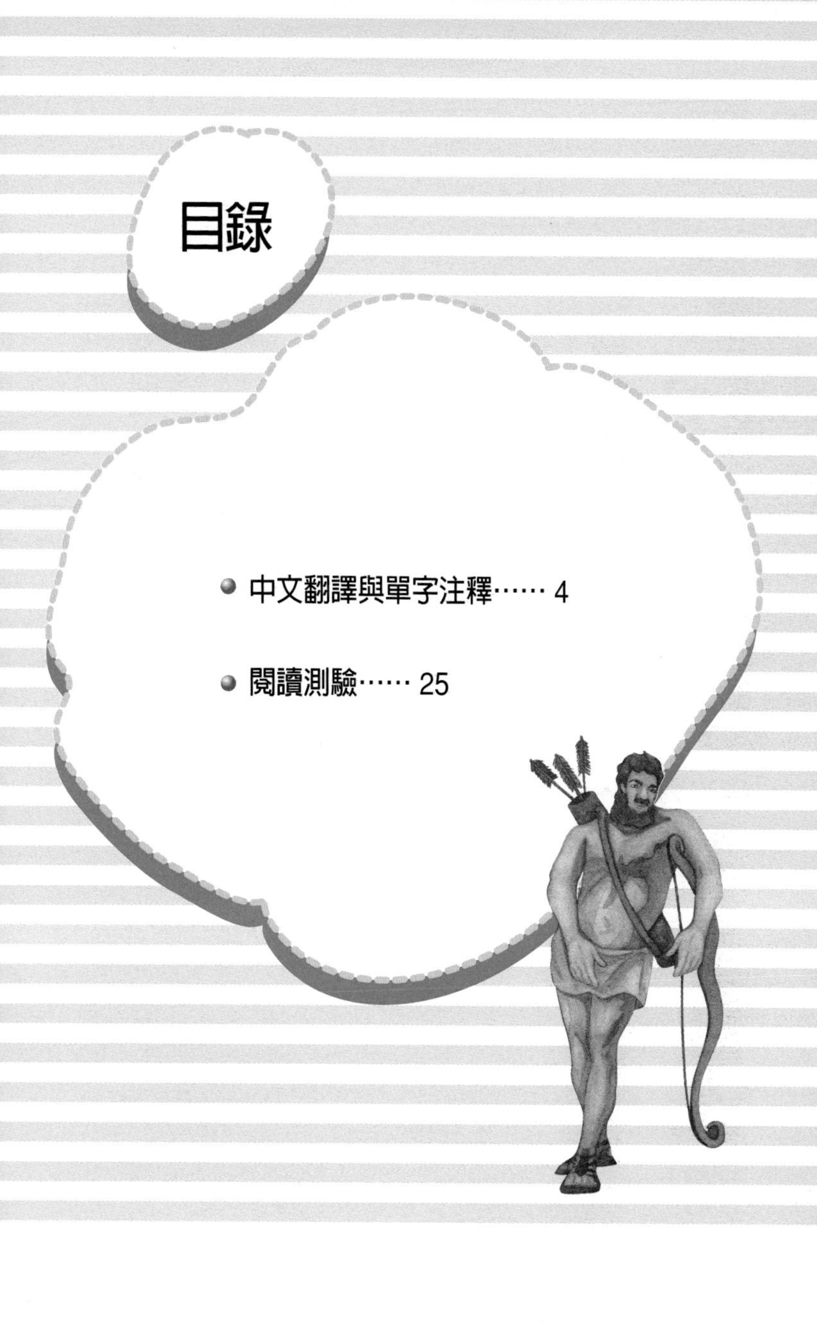

目錄

大力士英雄海克力斯

p. 8

希臘英雄海克力斯名揚四海，
他的母親是凡人公主愛克美娜，
父親是眾神之王宙斯。
海克力斯因此擁有特別的神力。

一日，女神赫拉派遣了兩條大蛇，
前來殺害海克力斯，
蛇卻反被海克力斯所擊斃。

- **famous** [ˋfeɪ.məs] 有名的；著名的
- **Greek** [gri:k] 希臘的
- **hero** [ˋhɪr.oʊ] 英雄；勇士
- **human** [ˋhju:mən] 人類的
- **princess** [prɪnˋses] 公主
- **special** [ˋspeʃ.əl] 特殊的；與眾不同的

海克力斯長大之後，
成就了許多偉大的事蹟。
他身上攜帶弓箭，是一名神射手，
也是世界上最強壯的人。
他娶了一位名叫美加拉的嬌妻，
他們育有子女，一家人和樂融融。

- **grew** [gru:] 成長；發育（grow的過去式）
- **older** [oʊldə] 較（old的比較級）
- **shot** [ʃɑ:t] 射手
- **bow** [baʊ] 弓
- **arrow** [ˋer.oʊ] 箭
- **strongest** [strɑ:gɪst] 最強健的（strong強壯的，stronger較強壯的）
- **married** [ˋmer.id] 和……結婚

p. 10

女神赫拉憎恨海克力斯，
便發下毒咒讓他身遭厄運。
一天夜裡，她對海克力斯施魔法，
讓他發了失心瘋。
他打死了自己的愛妻和子女，
還有許多其他人。

- **hate** [heɪt] 憎恨；嫌惡
- **luck** [lʌk] 運氣
- **magic** [`mædʒ.ɪk] 魔法
- **crazy** [`kreɪ.zi] 發狂的；發瘋的
- **suddenly** [`sʌd.ə.li] 突然地

p. 11

三日之後，海克力斯清醒過來。
他哀傷至極，
便向天神祈禱，祈求幫助。

但赫拉還不肯罷休，
她說：「海克力斯，
你去找尤里士修斯國王，
為他效命吧。」

- **normal** [`nɔ:r.məl] 正常的；常態的（指精神狀態）
- **upset** [ʌp`set] 苦惱的；心煩意亂的
- **pray** [preɪ] 禱告
- **hurt** [hɜ:t] 使痛苦；傷害
- **land** [lænd] 土地
- **work** [wɜ:k] 工作

海克力斯的十二件苦差役

海克力斯來到尤里士修斯的國度。
海克力斯說：「國王陛下，
「我必須完成您的所有指示。」
國王以爲海克力斯來意不善，
想要弒王篡位。他思忖良久，
說道：「你必須爲我完成十二項任務，
待完成任務，你就可以重獲自由。」

- **twelve** [twelv]
  十二（個）的
- **labor** [ˋleɪ.bɚ]
  （體力或腦力）工作
- **arrive at** [əˋraɪv æt]
  到達；抵達
- **kingdom** [ˋkɪŋdəm]
  君主的國土；王土
- **everything** [ˋev.ri.θɪŋ]
  任何事情
- **thought** [θɑ:t]
  思考；考慮
- **must** [mʌst]
  必須；應當
- **finish** [ˋɪn.ɪʃ]
  結束；完成
- **set free** [set fri:] 釋放

「第一項任務是什麼？」
海克力斯問道。
國王答道：「在奈米亞山谷，
有一隻獅子，獅子傷人無數，
你必須將牠擊斃，

- **first** [ˋfɜ:st]
  第一的；首先的
- **valley** [ˋvæl.i] 谷；山谷
- **skin** [skɪn] 皮；皮膚
- **travel** [ˋtræv.əl]
  遊歷；旅行

並把獅皮給帶回來給我。」

海克力斯來到奈米亞山谷。
人們警告他千萬不要靠近獅子。
但海克力斯並不退縮。

- **warn** [wɔ:rn] 警告
- **close** [kloʊz] 靠近
- **give up** [gɪv ʌp] 放棄

最後，海克力斯找到了獅子。
奈米亞之獅是一頭巨大猛獸，
牠怒吼一聲，衝向海克力斯。
海克力斯連續用棍子打獅子，
卻傷不了獅子。
最後，他徒手才將獅子殺死。

- **finally** [`faɪ.nə.li] 最後；最終
- **huge** [hju:dʒ] 巨大的
- **noise** [nɔɪz] 叫喊聲；喧嘩聲
- **ran at** [ræn æt] 向……撲過去；攻擊
- **club** [klʌb] 棍棒
- **didn't work** [`dɪd.ᵊnt wɜ:k] 無法奏效
- **instead** [ɪn`sted] 代替；頂替
- **was able to** [wɑ:z `eɪ.bl tə] 能夠……的（過去式）

p. 15

海克力斯榮歸，
全民歡欣鼓舞，
他殺了巨獸，
民眾為他歡呼。
國王很吃驚，
「海克力斯殺了獅子？
他是如何辦到的？」

- **return** [rɪˋtɜːn] 返回；回國
- **shout** [ʃaʊt] 歡呼（喝彩）聲
- **joy** [dʒɔɪ] 喜悅；歡欣
- **cheer** [tʃɪr] 歡迎
- **was surprised** [wɑːz səˋpraɪzd] 驚訝地（be surprised受驚地，surprise驚奇；意想不到的）

海克力斯回到城堡，
問道：「第二項任務是什麼？」
國王下令道：
「前往阿哥斯城，去找海德拉，
海德拉是一隻擁有九顆頭的怪獸，
找到牠，把牠給殺了！」

- **castle** [ˋkæs.l] 城堡
- **second** [ˋsek.ənd] 第二（個）的
- **must** [mʌst] 必需
- **country** [ˋkʌn.tri] 國家
- **Argos** [ˋɑrgɑs] 阿哥斯城（位於希臘東北部的一座古城）
- **monster** [ˋmɑːnt.stɚ] 怪獸；怪物
- **order** [ˋɔːr.dɚ] 命令

p. 17

這一次，
海克力斯與助手愛歐勞斯一起前往。
路程遙遠，他們最後抵達阿哥斯城。
九頭蛇怪朝海克力斯衝來，
海克力斯用棍子攻擊牠的頭，
擊落了其中一個蛇頭。
未料，斷頭之處，
卻重新長出了兩個蛇頭來。
沒多久，九頭蛇怪有了二十個頭，
但海克力斯仍毫無畏懼。

- **helper** [ˋhel.pɚ] 幫助者
- **quickly** [ˋkwɪk.li] 迅速地
- **knock off** [hɑ:k ɑ:f] 打掉；敲掉
- **grew** [gru:] 增長（grow的過去式）
- **its** [ɪts] 它的
- **place** [pleɪs] 地方；場所
- **afraid** [əˋfreɪd] 害怕的；恐懼的

p. 18

「愛歐勞斯，快將火把拿來！」海克力斯喊道。
他將一個蛇頭擊落，
令愛歐勞斯馬上用火燒之，
讓牠無法再生出蛇頭。
最後，九頭蛇怪只剩下一個頭。

- **bring** [brɪŋ] 拿來；取來
- **call out** [kɑ:l aʊt] 呼救；大聲喊出
- **burn** [bɜ:n] 燒
- **grow back** [groʊ bæk] 長回來；重新長出
- **only** [ˋoʊn.li] 只有

「最後這個蛇頭是打不死的。」
海克力斯說。
他舉起一塊巨石，朝蛇怪丟去。
巨石擊中蛇怪的頭，
把牠埋在巨石底下。

- **die** [daɪ] 死亡
- **lift up** [lɪft ʌp] 抬起；舉起
- **threw** [θru:] 扔；投（throw的過去式）
- **buried** [ˋber.i]（bury的過去式）

尤里士修斯國王很驚訝，
他說：
「接下來，去活捉席瑞尼夏公鹿！」

這隻鹿頭上長著金角，
牠是阿蒂密絲女神的寵物。
海克力斯在森林中發現牠。
然而，要活抓牠可不容易。
一年之後，
海克力斯抓到了這隻鹿。

- **catch** [kætʃ] 捕捉
- **deer** [dɪr] 鹿
- **golden** [ˋgoʊl.dᵊn] 金黃色的；金製的
- **horn** [hɔ:rn]（牛、羊、鹿等的）角
- **pet** [pet] 寵物
- **goddess** [ˋgɑ:.des] 女神
- **forest** [ˋfɔ:r.ɪst] 森林
- **caught** [kætʃ] 捕捉（catch的過去式）

「接下來，
爲我活捉厄瑞曼色斯山的大野豬。」
大野豬是危險的動物，
殺害過無數農民，破壞作物。
海克力斯與大野豬搏鬥，
大野豬逃到白雪皚皚的山裡。
海克力斯抓舉起大野豬，
將牠活抓交給國王。

- **boar** [bɔ:r] 野豬
- **alive** [əˋlaɪv] 活著的；沒有死的
- **dangerous** [ˋdeɪn.dʒɚ.əs] 危險的
- **farmer** [ˋfɑ:r.mɚ] 農場主人；農民
- **damage** [ˋdæm.ɪdʒ] 損壞
- **crop** [krɑ:p] 農作物
- **fought** [fɑ:t] 搏鬥（fight的過去式）
- **snowy** [ˋsnoʊ.i] 覆蓋著雪的；積雪的
- **grab** [græb] 用手抓握

「接下來我該讓海克力斯做什麼呢？」
國王心忖。
「我得找個他無法達成的工作。」

「海克力斯，去奧吉斯國王那裡，
他養了三千頭牛，
擁有世界上最大的牛棚。
棚舍已有三十年沒有清洗，
你一定要在一日之內清洗完畢。」

- **over** [ˋoʊ.vɚ] 超過
- **thousand** [θaʊ.zənd] 千；數以千計
- **oxen** [ˋɑksn] 牛（ox的複數）
- **stable** [ˋsteɪ.bl] 牛棚
- **largest** [lɑ:rdʒɪst] 最大的
- **clean** [kli:n] 乾淨的；清潔的
- **in one day** [ɪn wʌn deɪ] 在一天之內

海克力斯來到奧吉斯國王處。
他面對著牛棚，
「呃！這真是噁心至極，
奇臭無比！」他說道。
他坐下來思考：
「我該如何清洗這些牛棚？」
他想到了一個法子，
「對！就這麼做！用河水來洗！」
他大聲說出。

- **phew** [fju:] 呸！；啐！（表示焦躁、不快、厭惡）
- **worst** [wɜ:st] 最壞、最糟（的事情）（bad不好的；壞的worse更壞的；更差的）
- **smell** [smel] 氣味；難聞的氣味
- **terrible** [sæt daʊn] 可怕的；駭人的
- **sat down** [sæt daʊn] 坐下來（sit down的過去式）
- **river** [ˋrɪv.ɚ] 河流
- **cried out** [kraɪd aʊt] 大聲叫出（cry out的過去式）

隔天早上，海克力斯把牛群趕出棚舍，
然後到附近的阿爾菲斯河，
往河裡扔石頭。
沒多久，河水開始改道，流入牛棚。
這方法奏效了！
河水把牛棚洗得乾乾淨淨！

- **let** [let] 使
- **go out of** [goʊ aʊt ɑ:v] 從……出來
- **nearby** [ˏnɪrˋbaɪ] 附近
- **threw** [θru:] 扔；投；丟（throw的過去式）
- **go throuth** [goʊ θru:] 通過某處；流過某處
- **work** [wɜ:k] 奏效了

但這還不夠，牛棚很大，
海克力斯需要更多的河水。
他來到潘紐士河，
同樣將石頭擲入河道。
沒多久，兩條河的河水一起灌進牛棚。
一天之內，牛棚就變得乾淨無比了。

- **enough** [ɪ`nʌf] 足夠的
- **need** [ni:d] 需要
- **both** [boʊθ] 雙方的；兩者的
- **flow into** [floʊ `ɪn.tu:] 流入

國王又給了海克力斯下一個任務。
「海克力斯，前往阿卡迪亞，
那裡的沼澤區，
聚集了史泰姆法勒斯怪鳥。
牠們殺害無數人類，
去把牠們消滅！」

海克力斯來到阿卡迪亞。
但是沼澤地危險重重，
他根本無法進入。

- **swamp** [swa:mp] 沼澤地
- **too** [tu:] 太……
- **could** [kəd] 能夠（can的過去式）

突然，雅典娜女神出現，
想要幫助海克力斯。
她給海克力斯一面鼓。
「把鼓敲響，驅散怪鳥，
等牠們飛上空中時，
就能趁機殺了牠們。」

- **suddenly** [ˋsʌd.ən.li] 突然地
- **drum** [drʌm] 鼓
- **play** [pleɪ] 奏鳴
- **fly** [flaɪ] 飛
- **away** [əˋweɪ] 遠離
- **in the air** [ɪn ði er] 在空中

海克力斯大聲擊鼓。
鳥群討厭噪音，
牠們往上飛，
很憤怒地望海克力斯衝過來。
海克力斯舉起弓箭，
射下所有的怪鳥，
完成了第六項任務。

- **loudly** [ˋlaʊd.li] 響亮地
- **hate** [heɪt] 憎恨；嫌惡
- **noise** [nɔɪz] 聲音；噪音
- **flew up** [flu: ʌp] 高飛起來（fly up的過去式）
- **sixth** [sɪksθ] 第六（個）的
- **shot** [ʃu:t] 射擊；射殺（shoot的過去式）

p. 30

海克力斯回到尤里士修斯國王那裡。
國王說：「海克力斯，
麥諾斯國王需要你。
在克里特島有隻公牛，
牠生了可怕的麥諾特爾怪物。
這隻公牛凶殘無比，
牠已經危害到人們了。」

- **bull** [bʊl] 公牛
- **island** [ˋaɪ.lənd] 島嶼
- **monster** [ˋmɑːnt.stɚ] 怪獸
- **scare** [sker] 害怕

麥諾斯國王和海克力斯一起來到島上。
麥諾斯國王說：「就是這頭牛，
請將牠驅離克里特島。」
海克力斯遂追趕公牛，
公牛迎戰海克力斯，
朝海克力斯噴出火焰。
但海克力斯還是抓到了公牛，
將牠帶離克里特島。

- **take away** [teɪk əˋweɪ] 帶走；驅離
- **chase** [tʃeɪs] 追趕；驅逐
- **fought** [fɑːt] 打鬥；作戰（fight的過去式）
- **breathe** [briːð] 呼吸
- **caught** [kɑːt] 抓住（catch的過去式）

接著，尤里士修斯國王要求海克力斯帶回戴歐米德斯的馬。
這些馬不吃草或穀麥，只吃人。
海克力斯向戴歐米德斯要馬，
但對方說：
「休想！休想帶走我的馬。」
兩人於是打鬥了起來，
最後，海克力斯獲勝。

- **ask for** [æsk] 要求
- **grass** [græs] 草
- **oat** [oʊt] 燕麥
- **won** [wʌn] 獲勝（win的過去式）

---

p. 33

海克力斯的下一項任務，困難無比。
他必須前往亞馬遜國。
亞馬遜是個女人國，
全國上下沒有任何男人。
海克力斯需將女王的腰帶取回。
他帶著一群勇士一同前去，
他們在海上航行了許久。

- **difficult** [ˋdɪf.ɪ.kəlt] 困難的
- **Amazons** [ˋæm.ə.zɑːn] 亞馬遜
- **nation** [ˋneɪ.ʃən] 國家；民族
- **belt** [belt] 皮帶；腰帶
- **queen** [kwiːn] 女王
- **group** [gruːp] 群
- **hero** [ˋhɪr.oʊ] 英雄
- **sail** [seɪl] 航行

Did you know?

亞馬遜人

亞馬遜是個女人國。
傳說中，
亞馬遜族裡都是英勇的女戰士。
她們擅長射箭，
有時也使用長矛戰鬥。
習俗上，她們只扶養女童，
男童不是被送走，就是被殺害。
她們崇拜的「戰神」是阿瑞士，
阿蒂密絲則是她們的「陰柔女神」。

- **tribe** [traɪb] 部落
- **warrior** [ˋwɔ:r.i.ɚ] 武士；戰士
- **spear** [spɪr] 矛
- **custom** [ˋkʌs.təm] 習俗
- **raise** [reɪz] 養育；撫養
- **female** [ˋfi:meɪl] 女性
- **either . . . or** [ˋaɪ.ðɚ] 不是……就是……
- **worship** [ˋwɜ:ʃɪp] 崇拜；敬奉
- **as** [əz] 像……一樣

p. 35

最後，海克力斯和手下來到亞馬遜國。
女人說：「這裡是男人的禁地。」
海克力斯回答：
「我們要求見女王，請爲我們引見。」
亞馬遜人盯著海克力斯，
見他的外表英勇強壯，
便帶他晉見女王喜波莉妲。

- **finally** [ˋfaɪ.nə.li] 終於
- **may** [meɪ] 可以；能夠
- **enter** [ˋen.t̬ɚ] 進入
- **look at** [lʊk æt] 看著；注視
- **look** [lʊk] 看
- **brave** [breɪv] 勇敢的
- **brought** [brɑ:t] 帶領（bring的過去式）

「你爲何而來，海克力斯？」
女王問道。
「爲了將您的腰帶帶回。」
海克力斯回答。
女王很欣賞他的勇氣，
便把腰給了他。
這讓女神赫拉很生氣，
她騙其他亞馬遜人說：
「海克力斯要將女王帶走。」

- **bring back** [brɪŋ bæk] 帶回
- **however** [ˏhaʊˋev.ɚ] 然而
- **trick** [trɪk] 欺詐；騙
- **take** [teɪk] 帶

亞馬遜人信了赫拉的造謠。
在海克力斯泊船的岸邊，
雙方展開了一場激烈的戰爭。
女王喜波莉妲在激戰中喪生，
海克力斯也很欣賞喜波莉妲，
因而爲她的身亡感到很難過。
他帶著女王的腰帶，
回到尤里士修斯國王的城堡。

- **believe** [bɪˋli:v] 相信
- **lie** [laɪ] 謊言
- **battle** [ˋbæt̬.l] 戰爭
- **near** [nɪr] 附近
- **castle** [ˋkæs.l] 城堡

「現在，前往西班牙，
把傑揚的牛帶回來。」
傑揚是隻三頭怪物，
牠還有一隻雙頭狗，名叫歐塞洛斯。
海克力斯帶走牛隻，
傑揚和歐塞洛斯在後追趕，
但海克力斯將兩隻怪獸殺死，
帶著牛隻回到希臘。

- **cattle** [ˋkæt̬.l] 牛
- **two-headed** [tu:-hed.ɪd] 雙頭的
- **ran after** [ræn æf.tɚ] 在……後方追趕（run after的過去式）
- **went back to** [went bæk tə] 返回到
- **back** [bæk] 回原地

國王下達命令：「接著，
為我取來希絲柏瑞妲的金蘋果」。
希絲柏瑞妲都是水澤女神，
她們負責保管赫拉的神奇金蘋果，
有隻巨龍負責看守。
海克力斯問了很多人金蘋果一事。
有一個人告訴他說：
「去問擎天神阿特拉斯吧，
他才知道。」

- **nymph** [nɪmpf] 寧芙（居於山林水澤的女神）
- **magical** [ˋmædʒ.ɪ.kəl] 神奇的
- **dragon** [ˋdræg.ən] 龍
- **watch** [wa:tʃ] 看守；守護

阿特拉斯是位泰坦神，
他將世界扛在肩上。
海克力斯向他問金蘋果的事。
阿特拉斯說：「沒問題，
但你必須幫我扛世界。」
海克力斯便幫他扛起世界。

之後，阿特拉斯帶回金蘋果。
但世界太重了，
他不想再扛了。

- **Titan** [ˋtaɪ.tən] 泰坦神族
- **held** [held] 支撐著；保持著（hold的過去式）
- **world** [wɜ:ld]
- **shoulders** [ˋʃoul.dɚ] 肩膀
- **held up** [held ʌp] 抬起（hold up的過去式）
- **because** [bɪˋkɑ:z] 因為……；由於……
- **heavy** [ˋhev.i] 沉重的

海克力斯說道：
「好吧，那就換我來扛吧，
只是，我需要一塊軟墊，
你能先幫我扛一下嗎？
我先去找一塊軟墊，
找到了就會回來扛。」
於是阿特拉斯代他扛起世界。
「謝謝你，阿特拉斯。」
海克力斯說罷，
就帶著金蘋果離開了。

- **cushion** [ˋkʊʃ.ən] 跪墊；軟墊
- **for one minute** [fɚ wʌn ˋmɪn.ɪt] 一分鐘的時間
- **left** [left] 離開（leave的過去式）

尤里士修斯國王說：
「這是你最後一項任務，
下去冥界，爲我帶回地獄犬。」
海地士爲冥界之神，
地獄犬是海地士的看門狗。
海克力斯來到守誓河，
只有死人能夠渡過該河。
但是船夫害怕海克力斯，
就帶他擺渡過河了。

- **last** [læst] 最後的
- **underworld** [ˋʌn.dɚ.wɜːld] 地獄
- **guard** [gɑːrd] 守衛
- **only** [ˋoʊn.li] 唯有；只有
- **cross** [krɑːs] 橫越；跨過
- **ferryman** [ˋfer.imæn] 渡船主；擺渡人
- **was afraid of** [wɑːz əˋfreɪd ɑːv] 對……感到恐懼（be afraid of的過去式）

接著，他找到了地獄犬。
地獄犬是隻三頭巨犬，
尾巴是一條巨蛇，
背上也長出許多蛇。
地獄犬想咬海克力斯，
但海克力斯因爲披著奈米亞獅皮。
在強韌獅皮的保護下，
因此毫髮無傷。

- **tail** [teɪl] 尾巴
- **back** [bæk] 背後
- **tried to** [traɪd tə] 試圖要……（try to的過去式）
- **bite** [baɪt] 咬

海克力斯和地獄犬大戰許久。
地獄犬最後體力不支，
由海克力斯取得勝利。
海克力斯帶著地獄犬渡過守誓河，
將地獄犬交給國王。
他說：「這是地獄犬，
我的任務完成了。」
「你可以走了，海克力斯。」

- **tired** [taɪr] 疲累的
- **across** [ə`krɑ:s] 橫越；跨過
- **finish** [`fɪn.ɪʃ] 完成；結束

海克力斯之柱石

海克力斯來到非洲和歐洲的交界處，
他往地下挖掘，
用挖出來的土造了兩座山，
這兩座山便稱為「海克力斯柱石」。
在西班牙這邊的山，稱為卡波。
在非洲這邊的另一座山，
稱為阿比拉。

另有故事說，
在海克力斯抵達之前，
那裡有一座巨山，
之後他將巨山劈成兩塊，
此後地中海的水，
便從兩山之間流入大西洋。

- **pillar** [`pɪl.ɚ] 柱子；墩
- **dug** [dʌg] 挖掘（dig的過去式）
- **were called** [wɚ kɑ:ld] 被稱爲
- **another** [ə`nʌðɚ] 另一種；另一個
- **broke into** [broʊk ɪn.tu:] 將……分裂打碎成（break into的過去式）
- **piece** [pi:s] 件；個
- **Mediterranean** [ˏmed.ɪ.tə`reɪ.ni.ən] 地中海
- **Atlantic** [ət`læn.tt̬ɪk] 大西洋

閱讀測驗

※ **閱讀下列問題並選出最適當的答案。**

1. 請圈選出正確或錯誤。

■ 海克力斯的母親是女神赫拉。

True　　False

答案 False

■ 海克力斯還是孩提時，就曾殺過一頭獅子。

True　　False

答案 False

■ 海克力斯殺了自己的妻兒。

True　　False

答案 True

2. 下面哪個女神討厭海克力斯。

(A) 阿芙柔黛蒂　(B) 阿蒂密絲
(C) 雅典娜　(D) 赫拉

(D)

3. 海克力斯必須完成幾項苦差？

(A) 10 (B) 11 (C) 12 (D) 13

答案 (C)

4. 海克力斯如何清洗奧吉斯國王的牛棚？

(A) 眾神幫助他的。

(B) 他用一桶水清洗。

(C) 他借用兩條河的水。

(D) 他沒有清洗牛棚。

答案 (C)

5. 雅典娜給了海克力斯什麼？

(A) 鼓 (B) 木琴

(C) 三角鐵 (D) 鋼琴

答案 (A)

6. 請圈選出正確或錯誤。

■ 海克力斯殺了厄瑞曼色斯山大野豬。

True 

答案 False

■ 亞馬遜族都是男人。

True 

答案 False

■ 地獄犬是隻擁有三顆頭的蛇。

True 

答案 False

7. 大力士海克力斯從亞馬遜國帶回了什麼東西？

(A) 一根棍子　　(B) 一頭獅子

(C) 一條腰帶　　(D) 一個鼓

答案 (C)

8. 請在空白處寫下正確的英文。

■ 戴歐米德斯的 ______ 不吃草或穀麥。

只吃 ______。

答案 horses, people

■ 阿特拉斯是一位 ______。

他的肩上扛著 ______。

答案 Titan, world

9. 請問海克力斯沒有殺了哪種怪物？

(A) 奈米亞之獅。

(B) 九頭蛇怪海德拉。

(C) 奧吉斯國王的牛。

(D) 史泰姆法勒斯怪鳥。

答案 (C)

故事原著作者 Thomas Bulfinch

Without a knowledge of mythology much of the elegant literature of our own language cannot be understood and appreciated.

缺少了神話知識，就無法了解和透徹語言的文學之美。

—*Thomas Bulfinch*

Thomas Bulfinch（1796-1867），出生於美國麻薩諸塞州的Newton，隨後全家移居波士頓，父親爲知名的建築師Charles Bulfinch。他在求學時期，曾就讀過一些優異的名校，並於1814年畢業於哈佛。

畢業後，執過教鞭，爾後從商，但經濟狀況一直未能穩定。1837年，在銀行擔任一般職員，以此爲終身職業。後來開始進一步鑽研古典文學，成爲業餘作家，一生未婚。

1855年，時值59歲，出版了奠立其作家地位的名作*The Age of Fables*，書中蒐集希臘羅馬神話，廣受歡迎。此書後來與日後出版的 *The Age of Chivalry*（1858）和 *Legends of Charlemagne*（1863），合集更名爲 *Bulfinch's Mythology*。

本系列書系，即改編自 *The Age of Fable*。Bulfinch 著寫本書時，特地以成年大眾爲對象，以將古典文學引介給一般大眾。*The Age of Fable* 堪稱十九世紀的羅馬神話故事的重要代表著作，其中有很多故事來源，來自Bulfinch自己對奧維德（Ovid）的《變形記》（*Metamorphoses*）的翻譯。

■ Bulfinch的著作

1. Hebrew Lyrical History.
2. The Age of Fable: Or Stories of Gods and Heroes.
3. The Age of Chivalry.
4. The Boy Inventor: A Memoir of Matthew Edwards, Mathematical-Instrument Maker.
5. Legends of Charlemagne.
6. Poetry of the Age of Fable.
7. Shakespeare Adapted for Reading Classes.
8. Oregon and Eldorado.
9. Bulfinch's Mythology: Age of Fable, Age of Chivalry, Legends of Charlemagne.